the forever sky

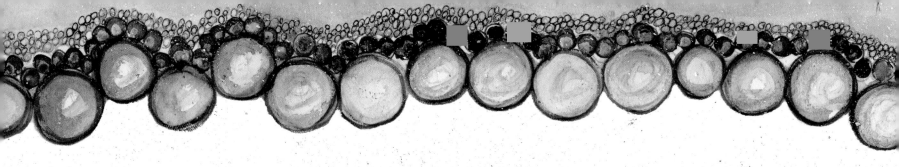

To my grandson Deklin *Niigaanii*, and to the memories of my daughter and son, Becca and Brady, who are somewhere beyond the Milky Way in the Forever Sky—dancing, dancing.—TP

To my mom, Sharon (Walsh) Lee, who went back to the stars in 2011.—ASL

mnhspress.org

The Minnesota Historical Society Press is a member of the Association of University Presses.

Manufactured in the United States of America.

10 9 8 7 6 5 4 3 2 1

♾ The paper used in this publication meets the minimum requirements of the American National Standard for Information Sciences — Permanence for Printed Library Materials, ANSI Z39.48-1984.

International Standard Book Number

ISBN: 978-1-68134-098-2 (hardcover)

Library of Congress Cataloging-in-Publication Data

Names: Peacock, Thomas D., author. | Lee, Annette S., illustrator.

Title: The forever sky / Thomas Peacock ; illustrations by Annette S. Lee.

Description: St. Paul, MN : Minnesota Historical Society Press, [2019] | Summary: Two young Ojibwe brothers, Niigaanii and Bineshiinh, look to the stars and spin stories, some inspired by Uncle and some of their own making, as they remember their grandmother.

Identifiers: LCCN 2018044663 | ISBN 9781681340982 (hardcover : alk. paper)

Subjects: | CYAC: Stars—Fiction. | Storytelling—Fiction. | Grandmothers—Fiction. | Death—Fiction. | Future life—Fiction. | Ojibwa Indians—Fiction. | Indians of North America—Fiction.

Classification: LCC PZ7.1.P4 For 2019 | DDC [E]—dc23

LC record available at https://lccn.loc.gov/2018044663

the Forever Sky

Thomas Peacock

Illustrations by
Annette S. Lee

MINNESOTA HISTORICAL SOCIETY PRESS

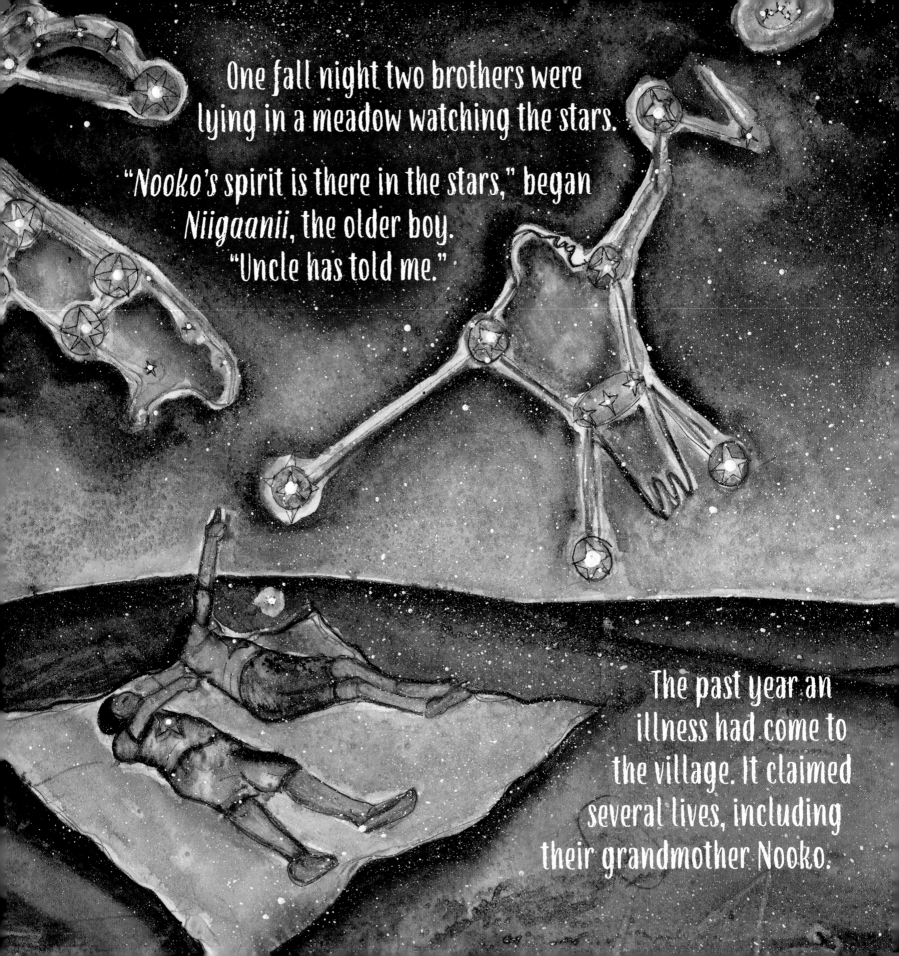

One fall night two brothers were lying in a meadow watching the stars.

"Nooko's spirit is there in the stars," began *Niigaanii*, the older boy. "Uncle has told me."

The past year an illness had come to the village. It claimed several lives, including their grandmother Nooko.

"Uncle said when Nooko's spirit left this world it went there."
He pointed toward the sky.

"I miss Nooko. I love her as big as the whole sky," said Niigaanii.

"Yes, the whole sky," said *Bineshiinh*, the younger boy.

After Nooko's passing, Uncle began taking Niigaanii to the meadow in the evenings. He had noticed how much the boy missed his grandmother.

"I will tell you stories so you know where she has gone," Uncle began. "Maybe you will feel less sad even though you will still miss her."

"The sky and stars all have stories," he said.

This is how Niigaanii came to know about the sky.

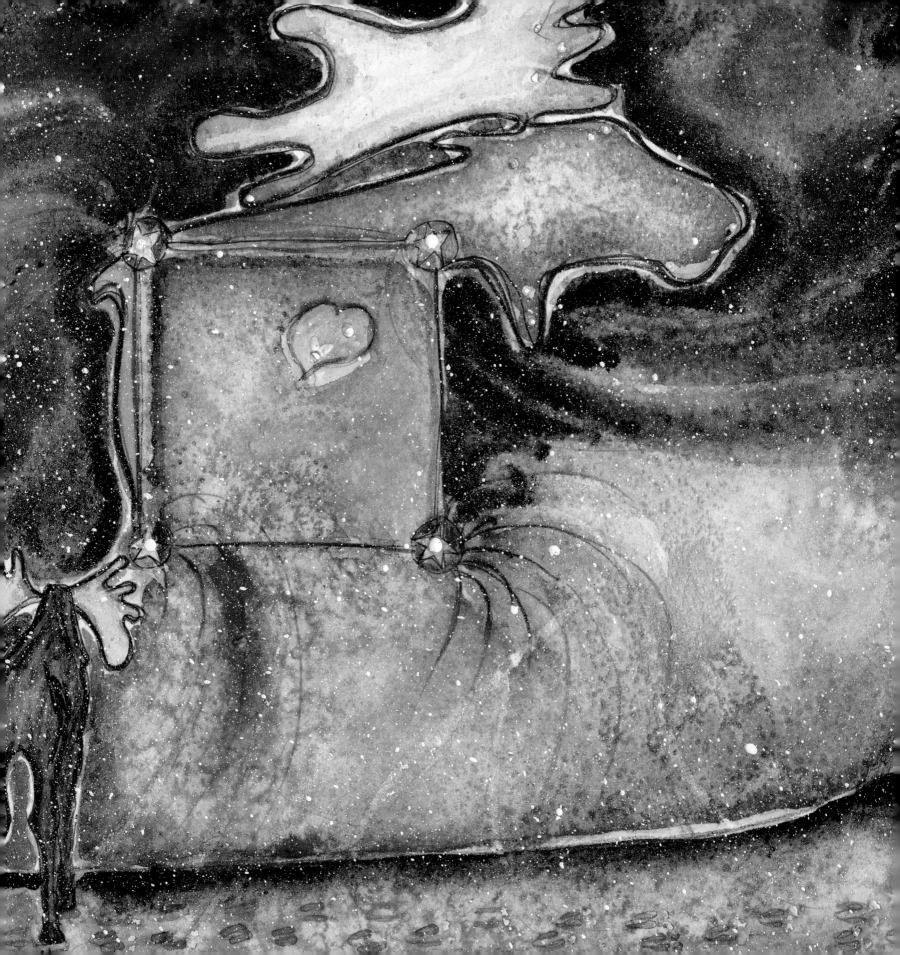

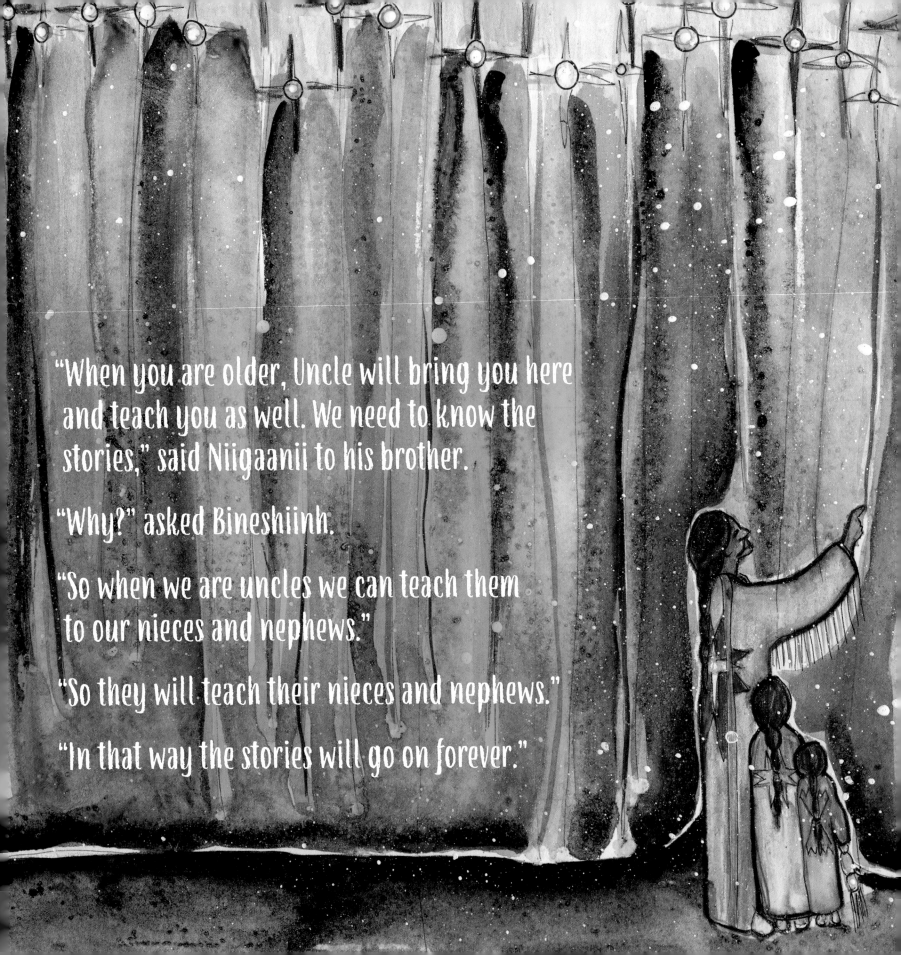

"When you are older, Uncle will bring you here and teach you as well. We need to know the stories," said Niigaanii to his brother.

"Why?" asked Bineshiinh.

"So when we are uncles we can teach them to our nieces and nephews."

"So they will teach their nieces and nephews."

"In that way the stories will go on forever."

The boys lay quietly for a long time, looking up at the sky full of stars.

Then Niigaanii spoke.
"The stars are too many to count."

"And the sky is so big it goes on forever."

"That is why we call it *Gaagige Giizhig*,
the Forever Sky."

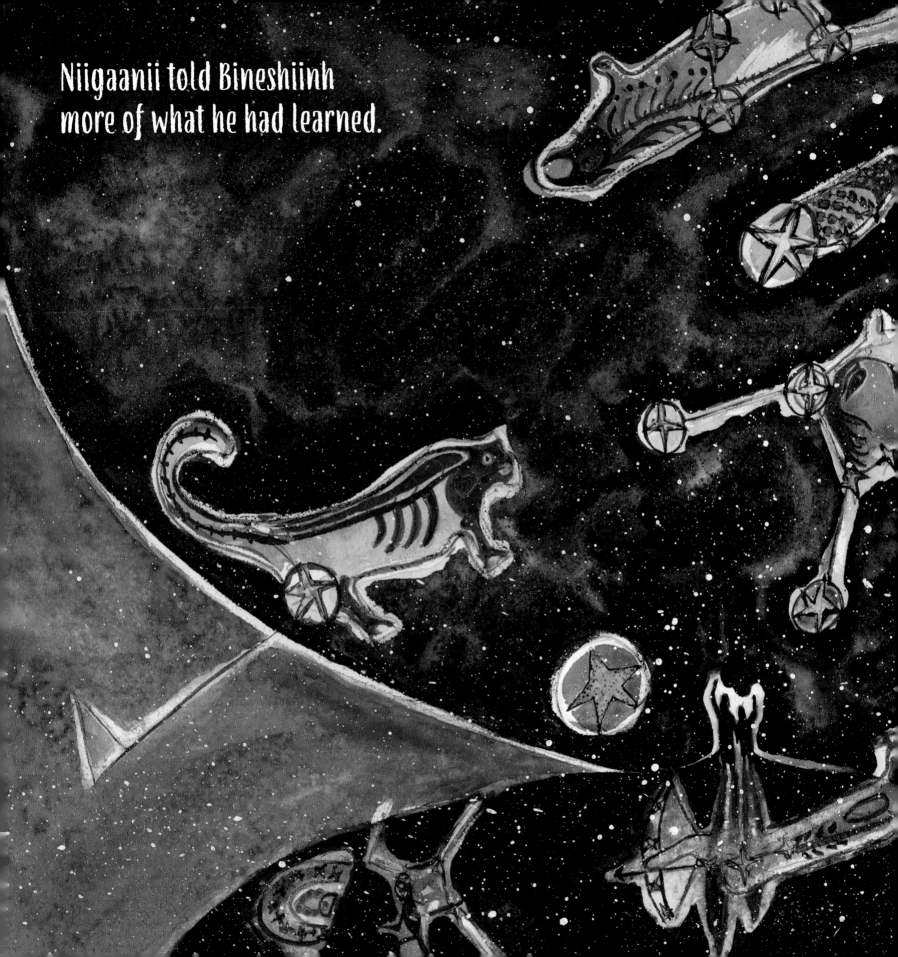

Niigaanii told Bineshiinh more of what he had learned.

How the stars form shapes of different spirits, animals, and things that live in the sky during each of the seasons. A moose. A panther. A fisher. A loon and a crane. A sweat lodge, a bather, and sweating stones. The spirit of Wintermaker. The hole in the sky. *Waynabozho*, who was the great teacher of the Ojibwe.

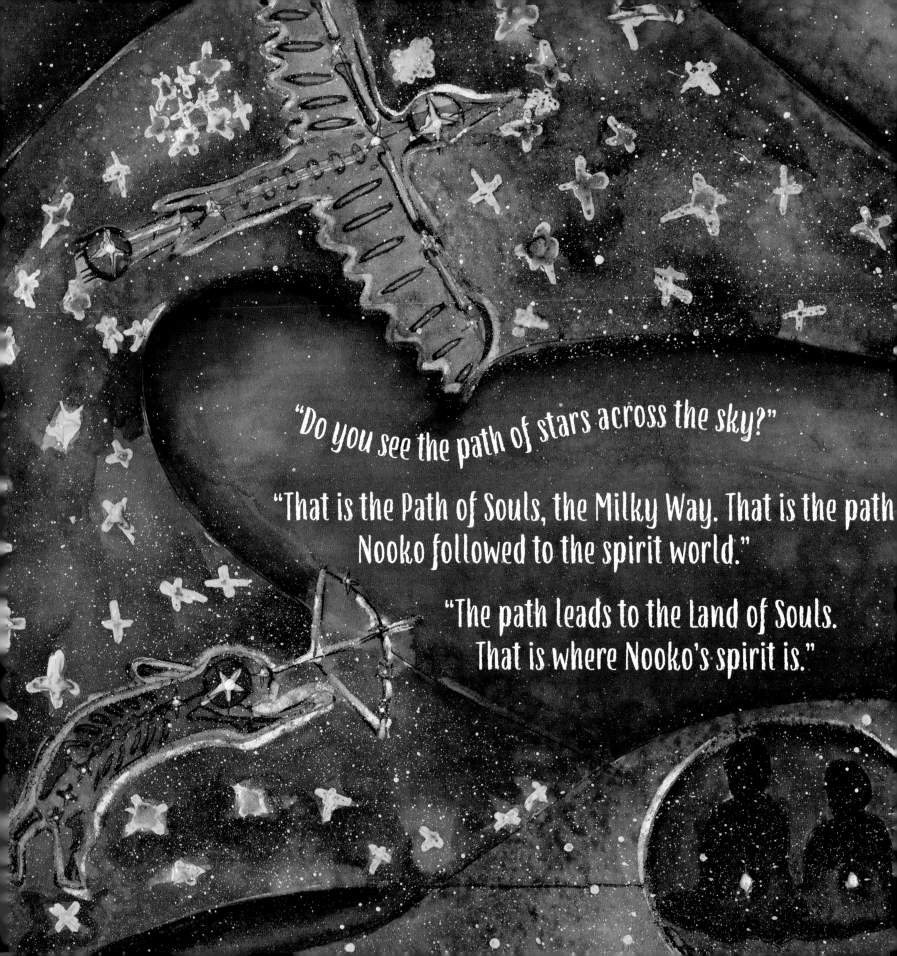

"Do you see the path of stars across the sky?"

"That is the Path of Souls, the Milky Way. That is the path Nooko followed to the spirit world."

"The path leads to the Land of Souls. That is where Nooko's spirit is."

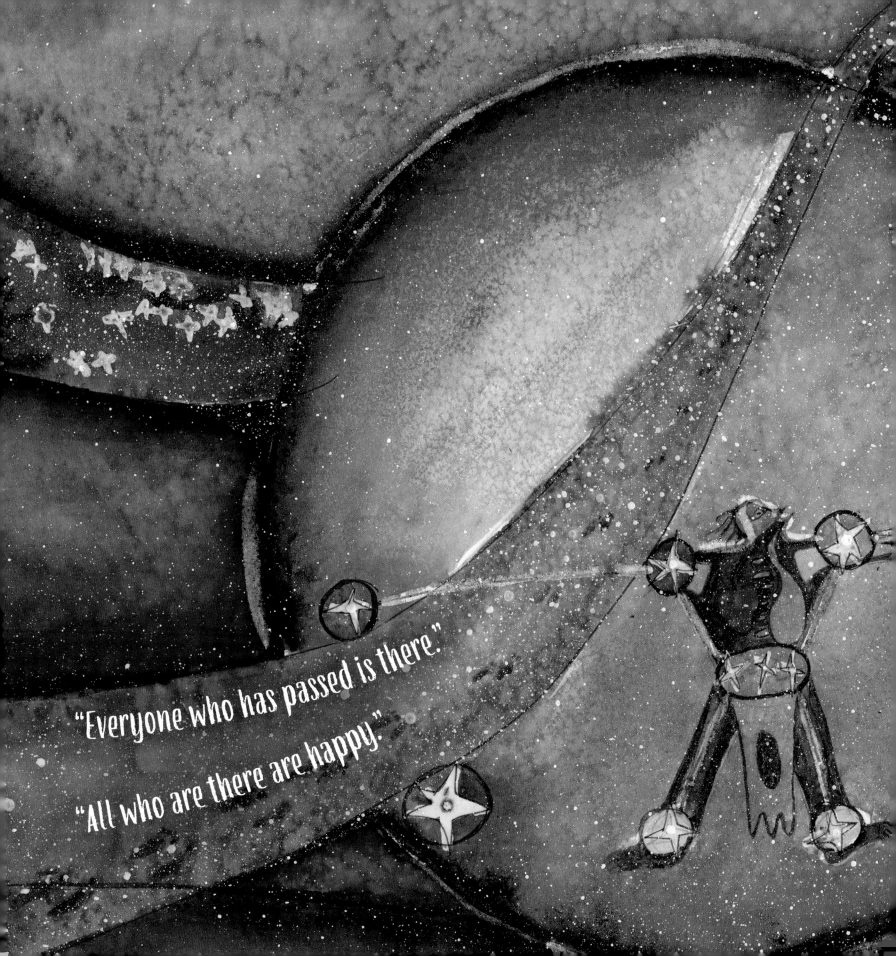

"Everyone who has passed is there."

"All who are there are happy."

For many nights the boys returned
to the meadow. And one special
night they stayed very late.

That night a beautiful
show of lights filled the sky.

"The northern lights," began
Niigaanii, "are the spirits of all of
our relatives who have passed on."

"Do you see them?" he asked.

"Yes, I do," said Bineshiinh.

"And what are they doing?"
asked Niigaanii.

"I think they are dancing," said Bineshiinh.

And that is what they were doing.

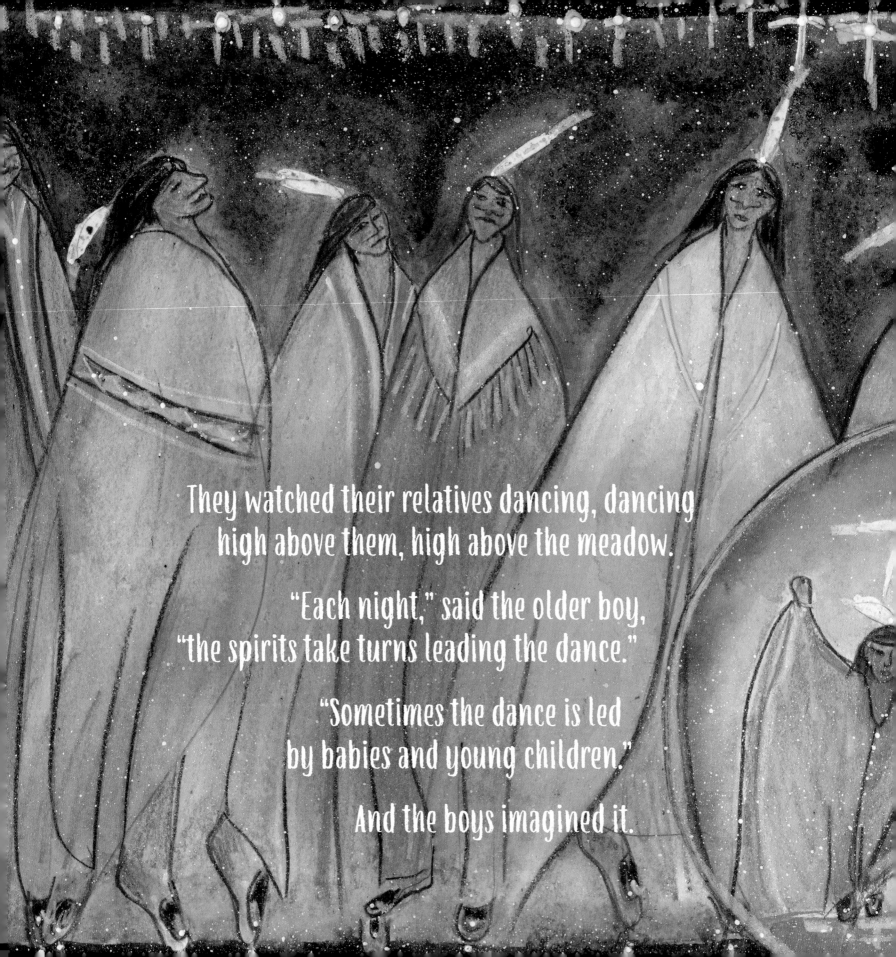

They watched their relatives dancing, dancing
high above them, high above the meadow.

"Each night," said the older boy,
"the spirits take turns leading the dance."

"Sometimes the dance is led
by babies and young children."

And the boys imagined it.

"And sometimes the dance is
led by those who were missing an arm
or a leg in their lives on earth. Or were blind or
could not hear while they lived on earth. In the
spirit world, all see. All hear. No one is missing
arms or legs."

And the boys imagined it.

"And sometimes the dance is led by the warriors."

"Warriors aren't just those who go to war.
Warriors are all people who do good things.
They visit the sick. They hunt and fish
and give food to the hungry. They
become mothers and fathers to
children who are without parents."

And the boys imagined it.

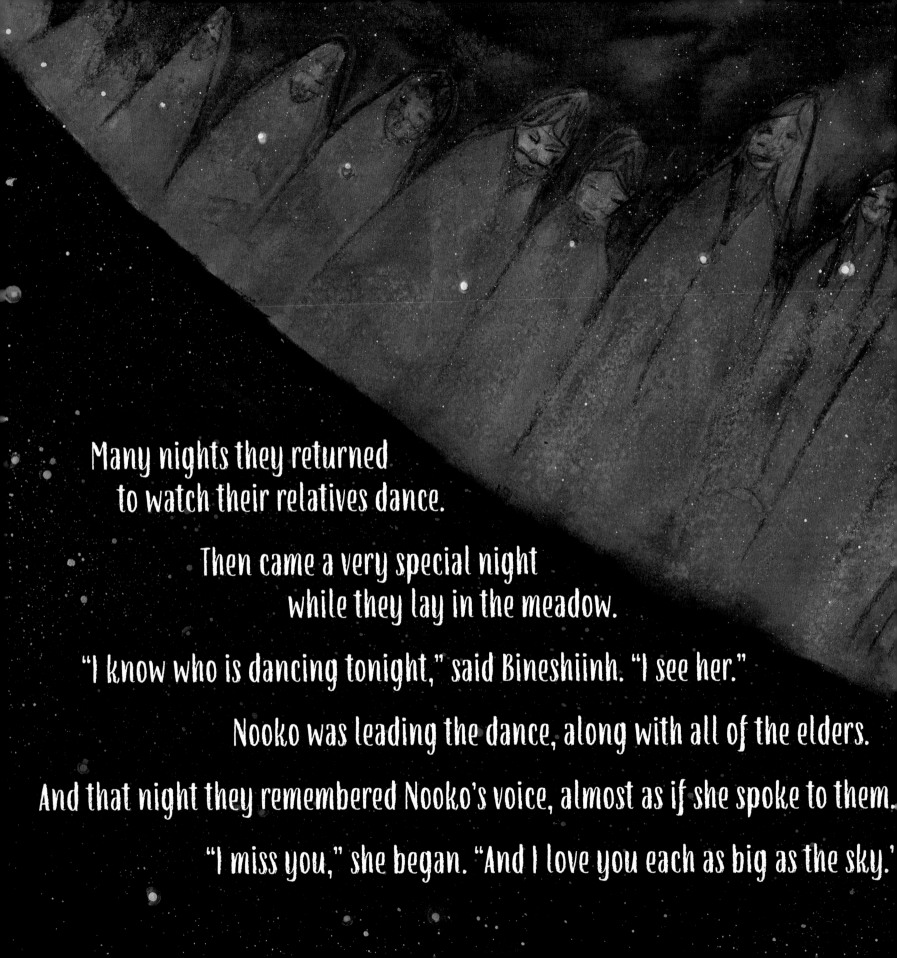

Many nights they returned
to watch their relatives dance.

Then came a very special night
while they lay in the meadow.

"I know who is dancing tonight," said Bineshiinh. "I see her."

Nooko was leading the dance, along with all of the elders.

And that night they remembered Nooko's voice, almost as if she spoke to them.

"I miss you," she began. "And I love you each as big as the sky."

"But I am happy here. My relatives who have passed on are here. My mother. My father. My grandparents, brothers, and sisters. My aunties, uncles, and cousins."

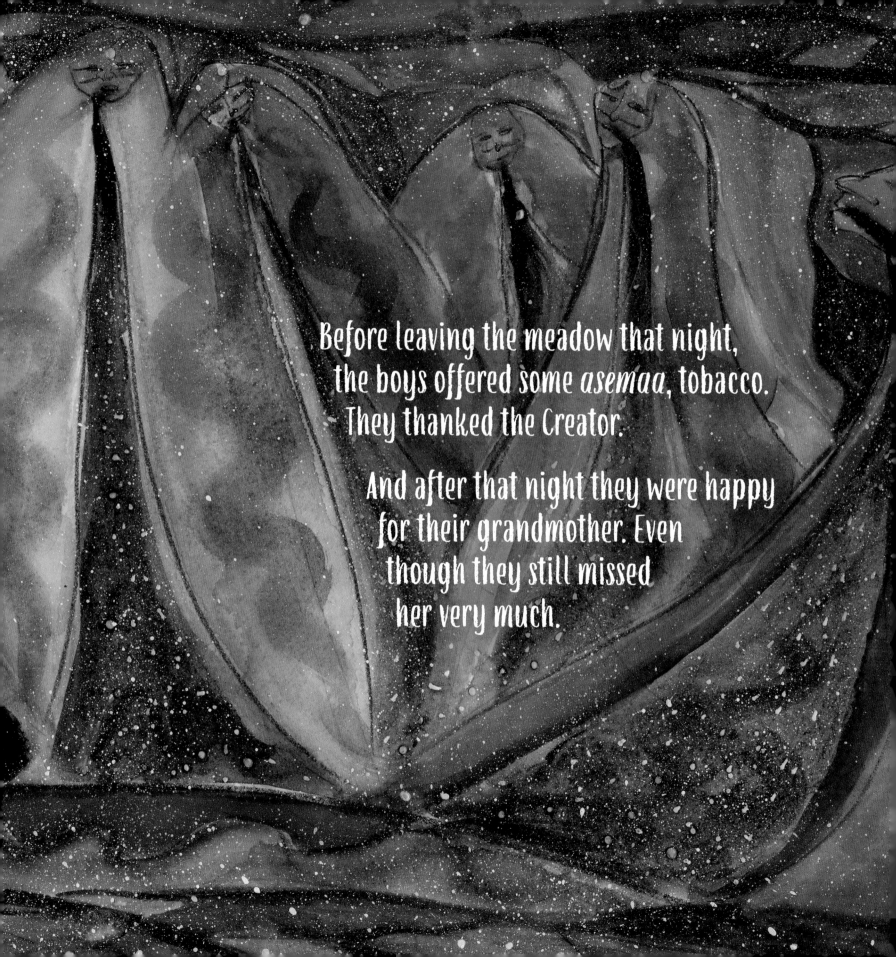

Before leaving the meadow that night,
the boys offered some *asemaa*, tobacco.
They thanked the Creator.

And after that night they were happy
for their grandmother. Even
though they still missed
her very much.

Several nights later they brought their mother and father and uncle out to the meadow. They all lay on their backs and looked up into the Forever Sky.

And they waited.

And waited. And waited.

Until the northern lights
began dancing.

Dancing.

Dancing.

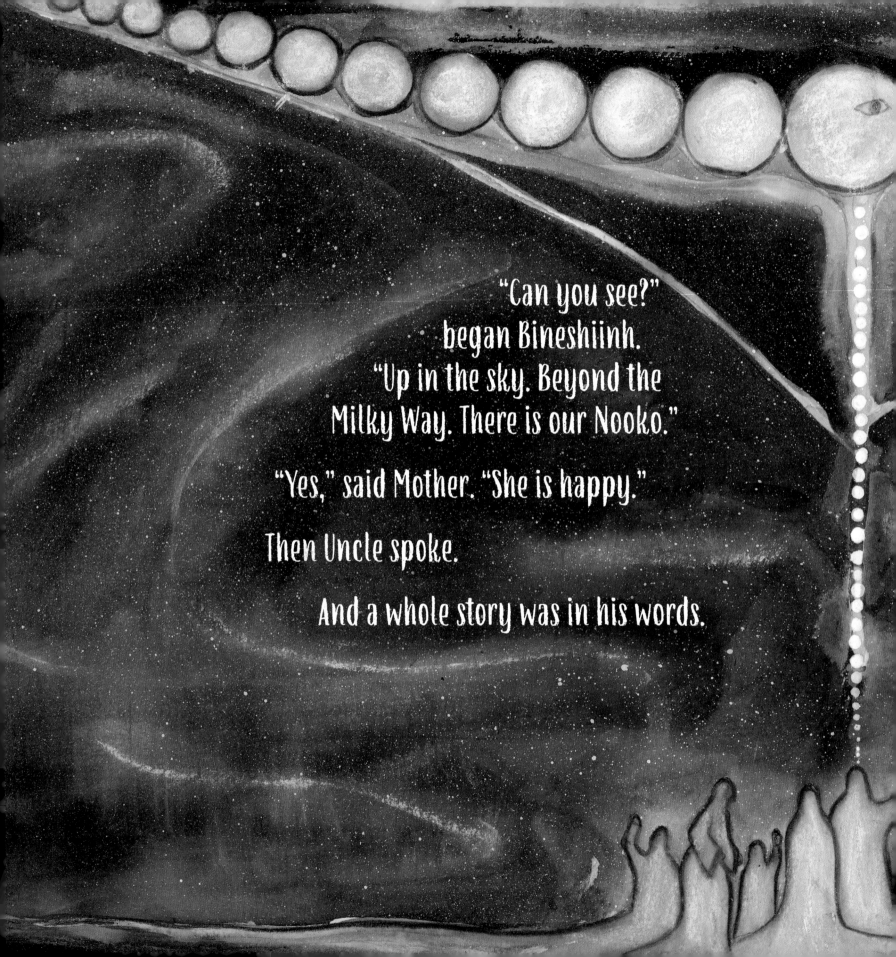

"Can you see?"
began Bineshiinh.
"Up in the sky. Beyond the
Milky Way. There is our Nooko."

"Yes," said Mother. "She is happy."

Then Uncle spoke.

And a whole story was in his words.

"She is a star."

"She is the northern lights."

"At night she dances."

glossary

Asemaa (ah-say-ma) tobacco

Bineshiinh (bi-na-shay') bird

Gaagige Giizhig (ga-zhi-gay gee-zhig) Forever Sky, Universe

Niigaanii (nee-gah-nee) to lead

Nooko (noo-ko) shortened, personal name for Nookomis, grandmother

Waynabozho (Way-na-boo-zhoo) the great teacher of the Ojibwe